Fat-free Recipes

Fat-free Recipes

Nevada Lampen

FABER & FABER
3 Queen Square
London

First published in 1977
by Faber and Faber Limited
3 Queen Square London WC1
Printed in Great Britain by
Latimer Trend & Company Ltd Plymouth

ISBN 0 571 11026 6

To my husband Fred

whose need and encouragement inspired me
to write this book

Foreword

It is with pleasure that I welcome and commend the publication of this volume. This is the first, and so far the only, cookery book which has been written to conform strictly to the principles of the 'fat-free' diet.

The amount of fat in the diet varies from one country to another, and is influenced by events. Among prosperous societies fat contributes 35 to 45 per cent of the total energy; in some poor countries the figure is 15 per cent or less. Before the last war, fat provided 39 per cent of the energy in the diet in Britain; as a result of the war, the figure fell to a minimum of 33 per cent in 1947; by 1967 it had risen to 42 per cent, and in 1970 was nearly 50 per cent.

All the available evidence shows that increased dietary fat intake, whether of animal or vegetable origin, is associated with a significant increase in the incidence of the so-called 'diseases of Western Civilization'. Studies of dietary changes among African races and the Esquimaux have shown that dietary fat intake has increased when these peoples have become more prosperous. When the Esquimaux leave 'native' areas and become 'urbanized' their dietary fat intake increases threefold. As their fat intake rises, these people become prone to the Fat Intolerant diseases so prevalent in those countries where dietary fat intake is already high.

My own work during the last 25 years has implicated excess

dietary fat intake as a major factor causing Fat Intolerance. In many patients this is associated with impairment of glucose tolerance, which may develop into maturity onset diabetes. In many more patients, this condition is associated with abnormal function in the 'smooth' or 'involuntary' muscle in blood vessels and in the alimentary tract. The symptoms of Fat Intolerance are relieved by strict adherence to the 'fat-free' diet, provided that irreversible changes have not already taken place as a result of too long an exposure to excess dietary fat intake. There is now ample evidence that among the conditions benefited by avoidance of fat are: maturity onset diabetes mellitus, cardiovascular disease, migraine, dyspepsias including hiatus hernia, peptic ulceration and gallstone disease, diverticulitis, 'colitis', 'spastic colon' and recurrent abdominal pain in children (the 'little belly-achers'), and obesity. In order to obtain relief, adherence to the 'fat-free' diet must be strict. The patient must avoid vegetable fat just as strictly as he or she must avoid animal fat.

Discontent with restriction of fat in the diet is not due to deprivation of fat. A national diet containing 33 per cent of fat supplies much more fat than is needed. The trouble is that food cooked without fat is considered to be dull and monotonous. Mrs. Lampen's book deals with this problem. This excellent collection of recipes will be welcomed by all patients and their relatives who have been advised by their doctors to avoid all fat that they can recognize in their diet. These recipes adhere to the strict rules necessary to safeguard the health of the Fat Intolerant patients and, at the same time, show how to restore variety and flavour to favourite dishes.

This book is a new departure, much needed. It will find an important place, not only in the homes of individual patients, but also in the hands of all dieticians, in hospital kitchens, in the offices of school meals organizers and, indeed, in the offices of all those concerned with catering for large groups of people. All who feed others have a responsibility for safeguarding the health of those they feed. Mrs. Lampen's recipes have been tried and proven.

Peter Childs
Plymouth

Acknowledgements

I would like to thank the Kellogg Company of Great Britain Ltd. for their permission to use their All-Bran recipe for the Fruit Loaf and *Woman's Weekly*, I.P.C. Magazines Ltd., for their recipe for Angel Cake.

Contents

Introduction

When my husband was placed on a 'fat-free' diet by his specialist, I realized that there must be many other people who, for medical reasons, were in the same situation as he. After a while the rigidity of the diet can become monotonous and often the patient will lose all interest in food.

As a result this book has been designed with these people in mind, and in the hope that by trying the fat-free nourishing dishes suggested they will once more find excitement and variation in their meals.

Most of the recipes would normally contain a quantity of fat or oil, but by adaptation a great variety of favourite dishes can be prepared and enjoyed to the full.

During the time that I have been cooking completely 'fat-free', I have found it advisable to make up the liquid powdered milk each day in a quantity sufficient to last the whole day, for cups of tea and coffee, making custard, etc., and any cooking. I cover it and keep it in the fridge ready for use. I try to plan the day's menu ahead so that I can make the exact amount needed.

While I find rice paper and vegetable parchment invaluable for lining dishes to avoid using grease, non-stick pans are without doubt a wonderful asset to fat-free cooking. In several recipes I use Golden Raising Powder in preference to ordinary baking powder, as it adds colour and makes the food look more appetizing.

For guidance the following table of do's and don'ts will be found useful.

YOU MUST NOT EAT OR DRINK ANY OF THE FOLLOWING, OR ANYTHING CONTAINING THEM:

Butter

Cheese

Cream

Ordinary or Channel Island
   milk

Margarine

Yolk of egg

Salad cream or mayonnaise

Kipper, mackerel or any
   fatty or 'oily' fish

Lard

Pork

Bacon

Ham

Sausage

Mutton

Liver

Suet

Pastry (unless made without
   fat)

Cake

Sponge containing any egg
   or egg powder

Biscuits: sweet, half-sweet or
   Cornish wafer

Chocolate

Toffee

'Ovaltine'

'Horlicks'

NEVER FRY. Do NOT use vegetable oil or fat, 'edible' fat or olive oil.

Look at the list of contents of every tin or packet: if they include fat, vegetable oil or 'edible' fat, DO NOT USE.

You CAN EAT OR DRINK THE FOLLOWING:

FAT-FREE (or SKIMMED) MILK
(*Beware*: NOT low-fat milk or milk-fat-free milk)

Tea and coffee

Alcohol

Cereals

Pastry, without fat

Porridge

Bread, white or brown, fresh or toasted

Sugar

Boiled sweets

Jam

Honey

Marmalade

Jelly

Tinned fruit

'Milk' puddings and junket made with fat-free milk

Custard made with egg-free powder and fat-free milk

White of egg

Meringue

Biscuits: cracker or water biscuits

Potatoes: boiled, baked (jacket), or mashed with fat-free milk, NOT roast, fried, chipped, mashed or treated with butter

Vegetables

Salad

Lean beef

Lean lamb

Lean tongue

Lean breast and leg of poultry

White fish, boiled, grilled (no fat), or cooked in wine

Fat-free soups

Fruit, fresh or stewed

'Marmite'

'Bovril'

Mint sauce

Tomato ketchup

Fat-free pickles

In spite of these restrictions, my husband and I are enjoying a varied, nutritious and exciting diet.

Nevada Lampen

Stocks and Sauces

Meat Stock

This can be made from stewing beef and/or beef bones, or oxtail. Allow 2 pints of water to each pound of meat or bones and add a little salt. Simmer slowly for 2 to 3 hours with the lid on the pan. When cold, skim off the fat and strain the liquid through a very fine sieve to remove remaining bits of fat. If the stock has jellied, remove the cake of fat and wash away any remaining particles of fat with warm water.

Bovril or Marmite Stock

One dessertspoon Bovril or Marmite dissolved in $\frac{1}{2}$ pint of boiling water.

Vegetable Stock

Any vegetables can be used, either alone or mixed. Slice and cook them in the normal way. Strain, and use the stock the same day.

Chicken Stock

This should be made in the same way as Meat Stock (page 19) using the bones or carcass of a chicken left over from other dishes.

Brown Sauce

Ingredients
1 small carrot
1 small onion
1 heaped tablespoon plain flour
1 pint meat, Bovril or Marmite stock (recipe page 19)

Method
Grate onion and carrot. Make a paste of the flour with a little stock, add onion and carrot and remaining stock and bring to the boil, stirring to prevent it burning. Simmer for 20 to 30 minutes. Strain if desired. If a thicker sauce is required, the amount of flour should be increased.

White Sauce

Ingredients
½ pint liquid powdered non-fat milk
1 level tablespoon cornflour or plain flour
2 drops Worcester sauce
salt and pepper

Method
Take enough milk from $\frac{1}{2}$ pint to blend flour into a paste. Boil
remainder and add the Worcester sauce, salt and pepper. Pour
boiling milk on to paste and stir well. Return to the saucepan
and simmer until it thickens.

Parsley Sauce

Ingredients
$\frac{1}{2}$ pint liquid powdered non-fat milk
1 level tablespoon cornflour or plain flour
salt and pepper
1 dessertspoon chopped parsley

Method
Blend flour with a little of the milk to form a paste. Heat remaining milk and seasoning until it boils, pour on to flour
mixture, stir well and return to heat and simmer until it
thickens. Before serving stir in the chopped parsley.

Bread Sauce

Ingredients
2 to 3 oz fresh breadcrumbs
1 small onion
$\frac{1}{2}$ pint liquid powdered non-fat milk
salt and pepper
2 or 3 cloves

Method
Peel the onion and gently simmer with the breadcrumbs, milk, cloves and seasoning for 20 minutes. Leave in a warm place until required. Remove onion and cloves, and stir before serving.

Alternatively, the onion may be finely chopped and only the cloves removed before serving. This gives a more highly flavoured sauce.

Mint Sauce

Ingredients
6 tablespoons vinegar
1 teaspoon sugar
1 tablespoon finely chopped mint
¼ level teaspoon salt
¼ level teaspoon pepper

Method
Sprinkle chopped mint with sugar and pour on 1 teaspoon boiling water. Leave to cool. Stir in vinegar, salt and pepper. Make the sauce some two hours before it is required so that the vinegar may take up the flavour of the mint.

Salad Dressing

Ingredients
3 rounded tablespoons powdered non-fat milk
2 tablespoons white vinegar

½ teaspoon mustard powder
1 teaspoon sugar
salt and pepper

Method
Put the sugar, seasoning and powdered milk in a basin. Add the vinegar gradually and beat well until smooth. Use the same day.

Soups

Mushroom Soup

Ingredients
¼ lb mushrooms
¾ pint vegetable stock
¼ pint liquid powdered non-fat milk
1 level tablespoon plain flour
2 level tablespoons powdered non-fat milk
salt and pepper

Method
Do not peel mushrooms but wash and chop them finely. Put vegetable stock into saucepan and add the mushrooms. Simmer for about 15 minutes until tender. Mix the flour and powdered milk into a paste with a little of the liquid powdered milk and pour on the contents of the saucepan, stir well, add the remaining liquid milk, return to the saucepan, season, bring back to the boil and simmer for a further 5 to 10 minutes. Serves four.

Clear Tomato Soup

Ingredients
¾ pint vegetable stock
½ lb tomatoes
½ teaspoon sugar
1 small onion
1 small carrot
1 teaspoon tomato ketchup
salt and pepper

Method
Put the skinned and sliced tomatoes, finely chopped onion and finely grated carrot into a saucepan, add sugar, tomato ketchup and stock. Bring slowly to the boil and simmer until tender. Add seasoning to taste. Serves four.

Thick Tomato Soup

Ingredients
as for Clear Tomato Soup (above) and in addition:
1 level dessertspoon plain flour
2 level tablespoons powdered non-fat milk
¼ pint water

Method
As for Clear Tomato Soup. When the soup has cooked, mix the flour and powdered non-fat milk to a paste with the water. Add to the soup to thicken, boil for a further minute and serve with croûtons of toasted bread. Serves four.

Leek and Potato Soup

Ingredients
3 medium-sized leeks
2 medium-sized potatoes
2 pints vegetable stock or water
1 dessertspoon chopped parsley
4 rounded tablespoons powdered non-fat milk
4 tablespoons water
salt and pepper

Method
Peel and slice potatoes. Wash, drain and slice leeks, using a little of the green part to give colour. Heat the stock or water in a pan and add the vegetables and seasoning. Simmer gently for 30 to 40 minutes. Pass through a sieve or liquidizer, return to the pan and add the powdered non-fat milk previously mixed with water to a paste. Reheat and serve garnished with chopped parsley. Serves four to six.

Pea Soup

Ingredients
½ lb split peas
1 small carrot
1 medium onion
a small piece of turnip
1 stick celery
2 pints water

salt and pepper
1 pint boiling water (for soaking peas)
¼ teaspoon bicarbonate of soda

Method
Soak the split peas for 12 hours in a pint of boiling water to which has been added the bicarbonate of soda. Wash and peel vegetables and cut into small pieces. Place in a pan with 2 pints of water and seasoning. Strain the peas and add them to the pan. Simmer for an hour or until tender, and pass through a sieve or liquidizer before serving. Serve with croûtons of dry toast. Serves four to six.

Lentil Soup

Ingredients
¼ lb lentils
2 large onions
½ small turnip
2 medium-sized potatoes
2 medium-sized carrots
2 pints water
salt and pepper
1 teaspoon mixed dried herbs
1 pint boiling water (for soaking lentils)
¼ teaspoon bicarbonate of soda

Method
Soak the lentils for 12 hours in a pint of boiling water to which has been added the bicarbonate of soda. Drain and rinse with cold water. Wash and peel vegetables and cut into

small pieces, and place in a pan with 2 pints of water, seasoning and herbs. Add the lentils, bring to the boil and simmer gently until soft. Pass through a sieve or liquidizer and serve with small croûtons of toasted bread. Serves four to six.

Onion Soup

Ingredients
4 large onions
2 pints water
¼ pint liquid powdered non-fat milk
2 rounded tablespoons plain flour
2 level teaspoons Marmite
salt and pepper

Method
Peel and cut the onions into small pieces. Place in a pan with water and seasoning and boil until tender. Mix the flour and Marmite smoothly with the milk and add to the soup. Boil well and serve. Serves four to six.

Fish

Baked Cod Steaks

Ingredients

4 cod steaks

14½ oz tin tomatoes *or* 5 to 6 medium fresh tomatoes (skinned)

1 level teaspoon grated onion

1 level teaspoon mixed dried herbs

1 level dessertspoon cornflour

2 rounded tablespoons powdered non-fat milk

salt and pepper

Method

Mash or slice the tomatoes together with the herbs and onion. Season with salt and pepper. Blend powdered milk and cornflour with a little cold water and add to the tomato mixture. Bring slowly to the boil, stirring continuously. Season cod steaks, place them in a casserole dish and pour tomato mixture over. Cover and bake in a preheated oven (375 °F or Gas No. 5) for 35 minutes. Serve with vegetables. Serves four.

Fish Pie

Ingredients
¾ to 1 lb cooked white fish
white sauce (recipe page 20)
1 lb mashed potato
¼ lb mushrooms (optional)
salt and pepper

Method
Flake the fish into a little thick white sauce. Season well and place in a non-stick pie-dish. Put a layer of potato on the top and lightly brush with liquid powdered non-fat milk. Bake in a preheated hot oven (425 °F or Gas No. 7) until potato is golden brown. More cooking is not needed as all ingredients are already cooked. Decorate the top with boiled mushrooms. Serve with peas and carrots. Serves four.

VARIATIONS
Thinly sliced tomatoes or shredded and precooked green or red peppers can be spread on top of the fish before adding the potato.

Cod with Wine

Ingredients
4 cod steaks
1 small clove of garlic
14½ oz tin *or* 1 lb fresh tomatoes (skinned)

1 medium-sized onion
1 level tablespoon plain flour
2 rounded tablespoons powdered non-fat milk
1 teaspoon lemon juice
2 tablespoons white wine *or* 1 dessertspoon Worcester sauce
1 tablespoon chopped parsley
salt and pepper

Method
Slice the onion thinly and place in a saucepan, add tomatoes, crushed garlic and parsley. Simmer until soft. Stir in the flour and powdered milk (made into a thin paste with a little water) to thicken. Add wine or Worcester sauce, lemon juice and a shake of pepper. Bring to the boil, stirring well, and pour into an ovenproof dish. Season the cod steaks and place them on the tomato mixture. Cover dish and bake in the centre of a preheated oven (375 °F or Gas No. 5) for 20 to 25 minutes. Serve with vegetables. Serves four.

Fish Cakes

Ingredients
1 lb cooked white fish
½ lb mashed potato
1 teaspoon chopped parsley
white of an egg
breadcrumbs or breadcrumb dressing
2 oz plain flour
2 tablespoons liquid powdered non-fat milk
salt and pepper

Method

Mix flaked fish and potato well together. Season with salt and pepper. Add white of egg to bind the mixture. Shape into eight balls, and flatten out on a floured board. Brush the cakes with the milk and dip in breadcrumbs. Then cook gently under a grill until brown and heated through. Serves four.

Plaice Fillets with Mushrooms

Ingredients
8 plaice fillets
1 tablespoon lemon juice
6 oz mushrooms
3 rounded tablespoons powdered non-fat milk
salt and pepper

Method

Season fish with salt and pepper and place in an ovenproof dish. Sprinkle with lemon juice. Wash and slice mushrooms thinly and add to the fish. Mix powdered milk with a little water until it is like a thin cream. Pour this over the fillets and cook slowly in a preheated oven (350 °F or Gas No. 4) for 35 minutes. Serves four.

Plaice with Orange

Ingredients
1 large plaice (filleted)
1 large orange

2 rounded tablespoons powdered non-fat milk
salt and pepper

Method

Wash the fish and season. Place in ovenproof dish. Mix
powdered milk with a little water into a thin paste and spread
over fish. Skin and remove pith from orange and then cut
into thin slices. Arrange orange on top of fish and cover.
Cook in a preheated oven (400 °F or Gas No. 6) for 35
minutes. Discard orange pieces. Serve with boiled potatoes
and peas or sweetcorn. Serves two.

Whiting Fillets and White Sauce

Ingredients

4 whiting fillets
3 level tablespoons powdered non-fat milk
1 dessertspoon chopped parsley
white sauce (recipe page 20)
3 tablespoons liquid powdered non-fat milk
1 teaspoon lemon juice
salt and pepper

Method

Mix the powdered milk into a paste with the liquid powdered
milk, lemon juice and seasoning. Spread over the fish,
sprinkle with parsley, roll up fillets and secure with cocktail
sticks. Place them in an ovenproof dish, cover with white
sauce and bake in a preheated oven (375 °F or Gas No. 5) for
30 to 35 minutes. Serve with vegetables. Serves two.

B

Meat

Beef Steak Pie

Ingredients
FILLING
1 lb skirt of beef
2 rounded tablespoons plain flour
salt and pepper
¼ pint water or meat stock

PASTRY
4 oz plain flour
2 rounded tablespoons powdered non-fat milk
1½ level teaspoons baking powder
a pinch of salt
water to mix

Method
Cut the meat into thin slices and dust with seasoned flour. Roll up and place in a pie-dish, adding the water or stock. If desired, a few tomatoes cut in quarters and/or sliced mushrooms can be added to the meat. Cover with foil and cook in a preheated moderate oven (350 °F or Gas No. 4) until tender. Meanwhile, sift together all the pastry ingredients and add enough water to form a soft dough. Remove the meat from

the oven and cover with rolled-out pastry. Increase the oven temperature to 425 °F or Gas No. 7 and cook for a further 20 minutes. This can be served either hot or cold. Serves four.

Meat Pie

Ingredients
FILLING
½ lb skirt of beef
2 medium-sized potatoes
2 medium-sized onions
salt and pepper
¼ pint water

PASTRY
4 oz plain flour
2 rounded tablespoons powdered non-fat milk
1½ level teaspoons baking powder
a pinch of salt
water to mix

Method
Mince or chop meat finely. Grate potato and onion, mix with the meat, add seasoning and water and cook gently until tender. When cold, line a pie plate with pastry (recipe as for Beef Steak Pie, page 34), cover with meat mixture and place another layer of pastry over. Trim edges and brush with liquid powdered non-fat milk. Place on the top shelf of a preheated oven (400 °F or Gas No. 6) for 20 minutes. This can be served either hot or cold. Serves two.

Winter Casserole

Ingredients
¾ lb lean stewing beef
2 oz seasoned plain flour
2 medium-sized leeks
2 sticks celery
4 teaspoons Worcester sauce
7½ oz tin butter beans
2 medium-sized carrots, sliced
salt and pepper
½ to ¾ pint water or stock (meat, vegetable or Bovril, recipes page 19)

Method
Cut meat into cubes and roll in seasoned flour. Place in casserole dish, chop vegetables and add to meat with water or stock. Stir in Worcester sauce, cover with lid or foil and cook in a preheated oven (325 °F or Gas No. 3) for 2½ to 3 hours. Serves four.

Chicken Casserole

Ingredients
1 large chicken joint
¼ lb button mushrooms
1 large carrot
1 large onion
2 oz frozen peas

salt and pepper
½ pint white sauce (recipe page 20)

Method
Cook the chicken portion in a roasting bag placed in a little
water in a preheated oven (350 °F or Gas No. 4) until tender.
When cool, skin and cut up into small pieces. Meanwhile,
chop the onion, mushrooms and carrot and boil together with
a little salt in enough water to cover them. When cooked,
strain and add to the chicken in a casserole dish, saving the
vegetable water to make the white sauce. Add the peas, and
pour the white sauce over all. Cook in a preheated oven
(400 °F or Gas No. 6) for 30 minutes. Serves two.

Curried Beef

Ingredients
1 lb lean diced or minced chuck or skirt of beef
1 large chopped onion
1 medium cooking apple, peeled and diced
1 level tablespoon curry powder
½ oz plain flour
1 level dessertspoon brown sugar
1 tablespoon sultanas
6 oz tin tomatoes *or* 4 medium fresh tomatoes
1 tablespoon sweet chutney
½ pint Bovril or meat stock (recipes page 19)
salt and pepper
long-grained rice (allow up to half a teacup per person)

Method

If using fresh tomatoes, remove skins. Roll the meat in the curry powder mixed with the flour, put all ingredients except rice in a thick saucepan or flameproof casserole and simmer gently with the lid on for about 2 hours, stirring occasionally, adding seasoning if desired.

The rice may be cooked as follows: Bring 3 pints of well-salted water to a fast boil. Wash the rice in cold water and tip it into the boiling water. Keep it boiling really fast for 10 minutes with an occasional stir. Then taste a grain or two. If it is soft but still 'chewable' it is cooked. Drain it and rinse quickly under the cold tap before putting it in a shallow dish in a cool oven or under a low grill to dry a little before serving. Serves four.

Cottage Pie

Ingredients
¾ to 1 lb minced skirt of beef
2 medium-sized onions, finely chopped
1 lb mashed potatoes
½ pint water or stock
½ oz plain flour
salt and pepper

Method

Place the meat in a pie-dish and add the onions and stock or water mixed with the flour. Season to taste, cover with foil and cook in a moderate oven (400 °F or Gas No. 6) for an hour or until tender. Remove from oven and spread mashed potato on top and brown under grill. Serves four.

Spaghetti Meatballs

Ingredients
1 lb lean minced beef
1 lb ripe tomatoes *or* large (14½ oz) tin of tomatoes
1 medium-sized onion, finely chopped
a small clove of garlic, crushed
2 level teaspoons chopped parsley
1 level tablespoon tomato purée
1 level teaspoon sugar
2 oz plain flour
1 rounded tablespoon sweet chutney or pickle
2 egg-whites
½ teaspoon pepper
1 bayleaf
a pinch of salt
8 oz long spaghetti

Method
Place garlic, chutney, parsley, minced beef and seasoning in a bowl and mix well together. Beat the egg-whites and add to the mixture. With slightly wetted hands shape mixture into 20 meatballs and coat lightly with flour. If fresh tomatoes are used, remove the skins and chop coarsely. Bring tomatoes and onion to the boil, adding a very little water if too dry, add tomato purée, sugar and bayleaf, and bring back to the boil. Add the meatballs and simmer for 35 to 40 minutes. Prepare a saucepan of fast boiling salted water and gently lower the long strands of spaghetti until they soften. Boil for 15 minutes. Drain, rinse and serve with the meatballs. Serves four.

Chicken and Rice Hotpot

Ingredients
1 large chicken joint
1 large tomato
1 medium onion, chopped
a little grated lemon rind
½ blade mace *or* ¼ teaspoon nutmeg
salt and pepper
2 oz long-grain rice
1 pint water or stock
½ pint brown sauce (recipe page 20) or alternatively any savoury sauce made with chicken stock

Method
Peel and slice tomato and place in a saucepan. Remove skin from chicken joint and cut into small pieces. Add water or stock and onion, lemon rind and mace (the mace should be tied in a muslin bag). Season and bring to the boil, reduce heat and simmer for 35 minutes with the lid on. Add the washed, uncooked rice and simmer gently with the lid on until it is cooked and all or most of the liquid has been absorbed. Remove mace. Transfer the contents of the pan to a warmed serving dish and pour over the hot brown sauce. Serves two.

Roast Beef and Yorkshire Pudding

Ingredients
1½ lb topside of beef

mustard
salt and pepper
½ pint Bovril or meat stock (recipe page 19)
1 teaspoon plain flour

Method
Trim all fat from joint, rub with dry mustard, salt and pepper.
Wrap meat in foil or place in a roasting bag and cook in
roasting dish in a little water in a preheated oven (350 °F or
Gas No. 4) for an hour. Remove foil, return to oven and
increase heat for a further 15 minutes. Make gravy with the
meat juice, stock and flour. Serve with boiled potatoes, green
vegetables and Yorkshire pudding (recipe below). Allow 30
minutes for Yorkshire pudding. Serves four.

Yorkshire Pudding

Ingredients
3 rounded tablespoons plain flour
1 rounded tablespoon powdered non-fat milk
1½ level teaspoons Golden Raising Powder *or* baking powder
a pinch of salt
4 tablespoons water

Method
Sieve dry ingredients together into a bowl, and add just
enough water to make a smooth batter. Beat thoroughly, add
the rest of the water and beat again. Pour the batter into a
non-stick baking dish of suitable size and cook near the top
of a preheated oven (400 °F or Gas No. 6) for 30 to 35
minutes. Serves four.

Lamb Stew with Dumplings

Ingredients
1 lb lean lamb fillet, diced
1 finely chopped leek
½ lb sliced onion
½ lb sliced carrot
½ lb sliced parsnip
1 small turnip, diced
2 tablespoons chopped parsley
4 large potatoes, diced
salt and pepper
1 teaspoon Worcester sauce
water

DUMPLINGS
2 rounded tablespoons self-raising flour
2 rounded tablespoons powdered non-fat milk
½ teaspoon salt
½ teaspoon mixed dried herbs
water to mix

Method
Arrange alternate layers of meat and prepared vegetables in a deep flame-proof casserole and season each layer with salt and pepper. Add just enough water to cover the ingredients, put on lid and bring to the boil. Reduce heat and simmer until meat is tender. Add Worcester sauce, stir and place dumplings gently on top of stew. Replace lid and continue cooking for 10 to 15 minutes before serving. Serve sprinkled with parsley. Serves four.

DUMPLINGS

Sieve dry ingredients together, and mix into firm balls with a little water.

Crunchy Salad with Tongue

Ingredients
¾ lb sliced tongue
1 small white cabbage or lettuce
2 medium-sized carrots
1 small bunch spring onions
½ small cucumber
1 large red dessert apple
2 sticks celery
1 red or green pepper
1 small bunch radishes
salad dressing (recipe page 22)

Method
Discard outer leaves of cabbage or lettuce and shred finely. Rinse in clean water and drain well. Peel and cut carrots into rounds. Peel and chop spring onions into ½-inch strips. Dice unpeeled cucumber. Core apple and cut into thin slices. Clean and slice celery thinly. Remove seeds and stalk from pepper and slice. Wash, top and tail radishes and serve whole. Arrange salad ingredients in salad bowl and serve with tongue and salad dressing. Serves four.

Lamb Curry

Ingredients
1 lb cooked lean lamb, diced or minced *or*
2 lb fillet or leg of lamb
1 large chopped onion
1 small tin tomato purée
2 tablespoons sultanas
6 to 8 crushed black peppercorns
1 large cooking apple, peeled and chopped
1 level tablespoon curry powder
1 rounded teaspoon plain flour
1 dessertspoon Worcester sauce
1 tablespoon sweet chutney or pickle
½ pint Bovril or meat stock (recipes page 19)
salt and pepper
long grain rice. Allow up to ½ teacup per person

Method
If using fresh meat, remove from the bone, trim off all fat and
dice the lean meat. The bones can be used for making stock
(see page 19).

Roll the meat in the curry powder and flour till thoroughly
coated. Place in a heavy-based pan or flameproof casserole
with all other ingredients except the rice. Bring slowly to the
boil, stirring occasionally, and simmer with the lid on till
meat is really tender. With fresh meat this may take 2 hours.
Add seasoning as desired, and more stock if necessary. Serve
with rice (prepared as for Curried Beef, page 38). Serves four.

Meat and Vegetable Pie

Ingredients

FILLING

1 lb lean chuck or skirt of beef
3 medium-sized potatoes
1 small turnip or swede
1 large onion
salt and pepper
a little gravy browning
water

PASTRY

4 oz plain flour
2 rounded tablespoons powdered non-fat milk
1½ level teaspoons baking powder
a pinch of salt
water to mix

Method

Cut the meat into small pieces and place in a saucepan. Peel
and chop potatoes, turnip or swede and onion finely and add
seasoning. Mix gravy browning with a little water, add to
pan, plus additional water to keep mixture from burning.
Stir often and when tender turn into an ovenproof dish and
cover with pastry (recipe as for Beef Steak Pie, page 34). Bake
in a preheated oven (400 °F or Gas No. 6) for about 20
minutes. Serve with a green vegetable. Serves four.

Grilled Steak with Onion Gravy

Ingredients
4 fillet steaks
1 rounded tablespoon plain flour seasoned with salt and pepper
½ pint Bovril stock (recipe page 19)
1 rounded teaspoon plain flour for thickening the gravy
1 large sliced onion
salt and pepper
a few drops Worcester sauce

Method
Trim off fat from the steak, wash, dry and dust with seasoned flour. Place under a hot grill, turning often so as not to harden the steak. Meanwhile prepare the thickened Bovril stock and put into a saucepan and bring to the boil. Add the finely sliced onion and seasoning and simmer until the onion is soft. Sprinkle a few drops of Worcester sauce into the gravy. Serve with boiled potatoes and peas. Serves four.

Roast Lamb with Mint Sauce

Ingredients
1 medium-sized leg of lamb
1 rounded tablespoon plain flour seasoned with salt and
   pepper
2 tablespoons redcurrant jelly
½ pint Bovril stock (recipe page 19)
1 rounded teaspoon plain flour (for thickening stock)

Method

Trim fat from lamb and rub all over with seasoned flour. Cook as for Roast Beef (page 40). Just before serving, make the thickened Bovril stock, add redcurrant jelly and baste meat. Serve with boiled or mashed potatoes, green vegetables and mint sauce (recipe page 22). Serves four.

Roast Chicken with Stuffing

Ingredients
4 lb chicken
salt and pepper
1 rounded teaspoon cornflour
1 teaspoon gravy powder
½ pint vegetable stock

STUFFING
½ small loaf of fresh breadcrumbs (about 5 oz)
2 oz dried onion *or* 1 large fresh onion, peeled and sliced
1 dessertspoon dried sage
½ teaspoon dried mixed herbs
2 rounded tablespoons powdered non-fat milk
a little lemon juice and/or grated lemon rind
salt and pepper
water to mix

Method

Remove any fat from inside chicken. Wash and dry and stuff with ingredients listed above moistened with a little water. Rub chicken all over with salt and pepper and place in a roasting bag in a dish of water. Bake in a preheated oven

(350 °F or Gas No. 4) for 1½ hours or until chicken is tender, increasing heat for the last 15 minutes. Make gravy with cornflour, gravy powder and vegetable stock. Remove skin from chicken and serve with boiled or mashed potatoes, carrots, a green vegetable and bread sauce (recipe page 21). Serves four.

Under Roast

Ingredients
1 lb braising or best stewing beef
2 lb potatoes, peeled and sliced
a pinch of dried herbs (optional)
salt and pepper
½ pint Bovril or meat stock (recipe page 19)
1 rounded teaspoon plain flour

Method
Trim fat off meat and cut into four thin slices. Arrange these in the bottom of a baking dish and sprinkle with herbs, if desired. Pour over the thickened Bovril stock and arrange potatoes on top. Cover with foil and cook in a preheated oven (400 °F or Gas No. 6) for 1¼ hours. Remove foil and increase heat in order to brown potatoes. Serve with mashed turnip and green vegetables. Serves four.

Meat, Chives and Egg Pie

Ingredients
¾ lb skirt of beef
3 egg-whites
a little liquid powdered non-fat milk
a bunch of chives, cleaned and chopped
salt and pepper

Method
Mince the meat or chop it finely and cook in a small amount of water until tender. Leave to cool. Line a pie plate with pastry (as for Beef Steak Pie, page 34). Beat the egg-whites gently and stir in with the meat and chives. Season to taste. Place on lined pie plate and cover with another layer of pastry. Trim and decorate with pastry leaves. Brush with liquid powdered non-fat milk and bake on the top shelf of a preheated oven (400 °F or Gas No. 6) for 20 to 25 minutes. Serves four.

Puddings
and other sweet dishes

Apple Pudding

Ingredients

FILLING
6 medium-sized cooking apples
4 to 6 tablespoons granulated sugar
½ level teaspoon ground cinnamon
2 tablespoons sultanas
3 tablespoons water
2 or 3 cloves

PASTRY
6 rounded tablespoons plain flour
3 rounded tablespoons powdered non-fat milk
2 level teaspoons baking powder
2 oz caster sugar
a little liquid powdered non-fat milk
a pinch of salt

Method

Peel, core and quarter apples and place in a pan with sugar, cinnamon, cloves and sultanas. Add a little water and bring to the boil uncovered. Simmer until cooked. To make pastry, sift the dry ingredients into a bowl. Add enough liquid milk

to make a soft dough. Roll out flat and line a non-stick basin
(1½ pint size). Fill with cooked apple and cover with pastry
lid. Seal basin with foil and boil or steam for 1 hour. Serves
four.

Pear and Honey Pudding

Ingredients
1 lb ripe pears
2 tablespoons clear honey
6 cloves
4 oz plain flour
1½ level teaspoons baking powder
¼ teaspoon salt
2 oz caster sugar
1 rounded tablespoon powdered non-fat milk
6 tablespoons water

Method
Peel, core and slice pears and place in an ovenproof dish with
6 cloves. Carefully add honey and mix well. Sift dry ingredients, add water and beat thoroughly. Pour mixture over
the pears and place dish on a baking tray. Cook in the centre
of a preheated oven (400 °F or Gas No. 6) for 45 minutes or
until golden brown. Serve with custard. Serves four.

Bread Pudding

Ingredients
4 thick slices bread

½ cup mixed dried fruit
a pinch of nutmeg or mixed spice
2 rounded tablespoons sugar
2 drops vanilla essence
2 level tablespoons custard powder
1 pint liquid powdered non-fat milk

Method
Trim crusts from bread, and dice. Soak the dried fruit in boiling water until soft and swollen. Put a layer of bread into the bottom of a pie-dish. Scatter a generous amount of soaked fruit over, then put another layer of bread over that. Repeat layers until the pie-dish is ¾ full. Do not press the bread down. To make the custard, reserve a little milk from 1 pint and mix with the custard powder to form a paste. Bring the remainder to the boil with the sugar. Pour this over the custard paste, stir, return to the heat and bring back to the boil. Add vanilla essence and spice. Stir well and pour over a little at a time until the bread and fruit have become saturated and the custard is completely absorbed. Cook in a moderate oven (400 °F or Gas No. 6) for about 30 minutes. Serves four.

Banana and Macaroni Pudding

Ingredients
3 oz macaroni pieces
1 pint liquid powdered non-fat milk
2 oz caster sugar
2 bananas
1 oz brown sugar

Method

Place marcaroni in a pie-dish with caster sugar. Pour on the milk. Bake in a slow oven (300 °F or Gas No. 2), stirring occasionally. When the macaroni is soft, remove from oven, peel and mash bananas and whisk into the pudding. Sprinkle brown sugar on top and brown under a grill until caramelized. Serves four.

Fruit Tart

Ingredients

FILLING

1 lb fruit (peeled and cored apple, rhubarb, etc.)
2 to 3 oz sugar (depending on which fruit is used)
1 tablespoon water

PASTRY

4 rounded tablespoons plain flour
1½ level teaspoons baking powder
3 rounded tablespoons powdered non-fat milk
2 dessertspoons caster sugar
a pinch of salt
water to mix

Method

Pre-cook fruit with a little sugar according to taste, and place in an ovenproof dish and allow to cool. Sieve the dry ingredients into a bowl, add water and make into a soft dough. Roll out quickly with as little handling as possible. Place on fruit, brush with liquid powdered milk, sprinkle with sugar and cook in the centre of a preheated oven (400 °F or Gas No. 6) for about 20 minutes. Serves four.

Fruit Sponge

Ingredients
FILLING
1 lb prepared fruit (cooking apples, rhubarb, etc.)
2 to 3 oz sugar (depending on which fruit is used)
1 tablespoon water

SPONGE TOPPING
4 rounded tablespoons plain flour
1½ level teaspoons baking powder
1 rounded tablespoon powdered non-fat milk
2 dessertspoons caster sugar
a pinch of salt
6 tablespoons of cold water

Method
Place the prepared fruit in an ovenproof dish with the sugar
and water. Sieve the dry ingredients for the topping into a
bowl, add the water and beat thoroughly. Pour slowly on to
the fruit and bake in the centre of a preheated oven (400 °F
or Gas No. 6) for about 45 minutes. Serves four.

Jam Pudding

Ingredients
4 rounded tablespoons plain flour
2 level tablespoons caster sugar
2 rounded tablespoons powdered non-fat milk

1½ level teaspoons Golden Raising Powder *or* baking powder
a pinch of salt
2 tablespoons jam
4 to 6 tablespoons liquid powdered non-fat milk

Method
Sieve the dry ingredients into a bowl, add the liquid milk and mix thoroughly. Place jam in the bottom of a non-stick basin and pour mixture over. Cover with greaseproof paper or foil and boil or steam for 1 hour. Turn out on to a warmed dish. Serves four.

Jam Pudding (alternative)

Ingredients
3 rounded tablespoons plain flour
3 rounded tablespoons fresh breadcrumbs
2 level tablespoons caster sugar
2 rounded tablespoons powdered non-fat milk
2 level teaspoons Golden Raising Powder *or* baking powder
a pinch of salt
2 tablespoons jam
a little liquid powdered non-fat milk

Method
Sieve the flour, Golden Raising Powder or baking powder, milk powder and salt together and add breadcrumbs. Mix well to a soft consistency with liquid milk. Place the jam in the bottom of a non-stick basin and add the pudding mixture. Cover with greaseproof paper or foil and boil or steam for 1 hour. Turn out on to a warmed dish. Serves four.

Pineapple Upside Down

Ingredients
1 small tin pineapple rings, drained
4 rounded tablespoons plain flour
1½ level teaspoons Golden Raising Powder *or* baking powder
1½ rounded tablespoons powdered non-fat milk
2 level tablespoons caster sugar
a little liquid powdered non-fat milk
a little apricot jam

Method
Sieve the dry ingredients together. Gradually add the liquid milk to make a runny consistency. Have ready a shallow ovenproof dish which has been rubbed all over with apricot jam. Place the drained pineapple rings in the bottom of the dish and pour the batter slowly over them. Cook in the centre of a preheated oven (375 °F or Gas No. 5) for 45 minutes or until firm to the touch. Serve with custard. Serves four.

Queen of Puddings

Ingredients
4 slices white bread
4 level tablespoons caster sugar
1 pint liquid powdered non-fat milk
2 tablespoons strawberry or raspberry jam
1 egg-white

Method

Trim crusts from bread and cut into medium-sized pieces to fit into ovenproof dish. Spread the jam on the bottom of the dish and then layer bread and half the sugar until all the bread is used, beginning and ending with bread. Pour the liquid milk over and bake in the centre of a preheated oven (400 °F or Gas No. 6) for 30 minutes or until firm. Beat the egg-white until quite stiff and standing in points, and stir into it the remaining 2 tablespoons of caster sugar. Remove pudding from the oven and cover it with meringue mixture. Brown under grill or return to hot oven (425 °F or Gas No. 7) for 5 to 10 minutes. Serves four.

Treacle Pudding

Ingredients

4 rounded tablespoons plain flour
2 rounded tablespoons powdered non-fat milk
1½ rounded tablespoons caster sugar
1½ level teaspoons Golden Raising Powder *or* baking powder
½ teacup mixed dried fruit
a pinch of salt
liquid powdered non-fat milk to mix
2 tablespoons golden syrup

Method

Sieve the flour, sugar, milk powder, Golden Raising Powder or baking powder, and salt together. Add the cleaned fruit and mix with about 6 tablespoons liquid milk. Place the syrup in the bottom of a 1-pint non-stick basin and pour the pudding mixture on top. Cover with greaseproof paper or foil and boil or steam for 1 hour. Turn out on to a warmed dish. Serves four.

Christmas Pudding

Ingredients
2 rounded tablespoons self-raising flour
1½ oz brown sugar
1 cup mixed dried fruit
½ teaspoon mixed spice
3 rounded tablespoons powdered non-fat milk
a few drops of rum or almond essence
½ lemon, rind and juice
2 oz fresh breadcrumbs
1 tablespoon black treacle
a pinch of salt
1 tablespoon marmalade
6 tablespoons liquid powdered non-fat milk
1 tablespoon brandy or sherry (optional)

Method
Mix dry ingredients in a bowl and add the finely cut lemon rind and juice. Next add the cleaned fruit, marmalade, essence, brandy or sherry if used, warmed treacle and enough liquid milk to make a stiff consistency. Thoroughly mix ingredients, place in a 1-pint non-stick basin and boil or steam for 1½ hours. This pudding will keep for three days and may be reheated by boiling or steaming for 20 minutes. Serves four.

Mincemeat

Ingredients
1 grated apple
1 tablespoon currants
1 tablespoon sultanas
1 tablespoon chopped glacé cherries
1 tablespoon chopped mixed peel
1 tablespoon sherry (or brandy, whisky, rum, as preferred)
1 tablespoon marmalade
1½ rounded tablespoons brown sugar
1 level teaspoon mixed spice
a shake of nutmeg
1 rounded tablespoon powdered non-fat milk

Method
Cook the apple with the sugar until tender. When cold, add the other ingredients, finally stirring in the powdered milk. Use within three days.

Mince Pies

Ingredients
4 rounded tablespoons plain flour
2 rounded tablespoons powdered non-fat milk
1 tablespoon caster sugar
1½ level teaspoons baking powder
a pinch of salt
water to mix
mincemeat for filling (recipe above)

Method

Sieve the dry ingredients into a bowl and add a small quantity of water to make a stiff dough. Roll pastry out thinly, cut into rounds and line the compartments of a non-stick patty tin. Fill with mincemeat and cover with pastry. Brush with liquid powdered non-fat milk and sprinkle with caster sugar. Cook near the top of a preheated oven (400 °F or Gas No. 6) for 20 minutes. Makes 8 to 10 pies.

Alternatively one large open tart can be made and decorated with twists of pastry. The cooking time should be increased to 30 minutes.

Currant Pancakes with Honey Sauce

Ingredients

2 rounded tablespoons self-raising flour
1 rounded tablespoon caster sugar
1 rounded tablespoon powdered non-fat milk
2 tablespoons liquid powdered non-fat milk
1 teaspoon custard powder
1 tablespoon currants
1 egg-white
a pinch of salt

Honey Sauce
Juice of $\frac{1}{2}$ lemon
1 tablespoon clear honey
1 tablespoon water

Method

Sieve dry ingredients together into a mixing bowl. Make a

well and add the lightly-beaten egg-white and enough liquid powdered non-fat milk to make a smooth batter. Lastly, add the fruit. Divide mixture into two and pour half into a 7-inch non-stick frying pan. Swivel the pan so that the mixture thinly covers the base and cook for 2 minutes each side over medium heat, until nicely brown. Serve with honey sauce prepared as follows:

Put honey and water into a small saucepan and stir well until hot, add lemon juice and heat through again. Pour over hot pancakes. Serves two.

Apricot Delight

Ingredients

15 oz tin apricots
3 oz fresh breadcrumbs
2 tablespoons apricot brandy *or* 4 tablespoons apricot wine (optional)
1 large egg-white
½ pint liquid powdered non-fat milk
1 rounded tablespoon caster sugar
2 rounded tablespoons powdered non-fat milk
1 rounded tablespoon custard powder

Method

Drain juice from apricots. Place the breadcrumbs in an oven-proof dish and pour over juice and wine or brandy if used. Mix well. Arrange apricots on mixture. Then whisk the egg-white, custard powder, sugar and powdered milk together, gradually adding all the liquid milk. Pour this carefully on to the apricots. Bake in a preheated oven (350 °F or Gas No. 4) for an hour, or until custard is set. Allow to cool before serving. Serves four.

Milk Jelly Whip

Ingredients
1 packet jelly (crystals or tablet)
½ pint water
½ pint liquid powdered non-fat milk

Method
Dissolve the jelly in ½ pint of boiling water and when cool add the ½ pint of milk. Leave to set. Then whip with a rotary whisk until the jelly is very frothy. Pour into individual dishes and when re-set decorate with fruit and whipped cream (recipes pages 85–6). Serves four.

Orange Baked Apples

Ingredients
6 medium-sized cooking apples
2 medium-sized oranges
1 oz glacé cherries
1 teaspoon almond essence
4 tablespoons clear honey
3 oz ground rice
1 oz caster sugar

Method

Wash and core apples, and run a sharp knife round the middle of each just to cut the skin and permit expansion when cooking. Peel the oranges thinly and cut the rind into thin shreds. Place the rind and honey in a pan and bring to the boil. Continue to cook for 1 minute. Remove any pith from the oranges and cut the flesh into very small pieces and mix with the ground rice, almond essence, chopped cherries and sugar. Fill the centres of the apples with the mixture and place in an ovenproof dish. Pour the honey and orange shreds over the apples, cover and bake in the centre of a preheated oven (350° F or Gas No. 4) for 45 minutes. Serve hot or cold. Serves four.

Orange Sundaes

Ingredients

¾ lb cooking apples
½ packet orange jelly (crystals or tablet)
1 small orange
whipped cream (recipes pages 85–6)
½ pint liquid powdered non-fat milk
glacé cherries and angelica for decoration

Method

Peel and quarter the apples, and cook in a little water, then sweeten and sieve. Divide apple purée into four sundae dishes. Cover with jelly made with liquid powdered non-fat milk. When the mixture is firmly set, top with cream and decorate with cherries, angelica and slices of orange. Serves four.

Tangy Apples with Sultanas

Ingredients
4 large cooking apples
3 level tablespoons orange marmalade
2 level tablespoons brown sugar
the juice of 1 small orange
2 tablespoons sultanas
1 tablespoon clear honey
whipped cream (recipes pages 85–6)

Method
Peel and thinly slice apples and put in a saucepan with marmalade, honey and sugar. Add the orange juice and bring slowly to the boil. Stir in the sultanas and cook until tender. Cool and serve with whipped cream. Serves four.

Pear Cream Jelly

Ingredients
1 packet lemon jelly (crystals or tablet)
2 or 3 cooking pears
¼ pint whipped cream (recipes pages 85–6)
¾ pint boiling water
glacé cherries and angelica for decoration

Method
Prepare a mould by rinsing well in cold water. Leave it wet. Dissolve jelly in boiling water and leave on one side until

thick and syrupy. Peel and core pears, grate coarsely and add to the setting jelly. Stir in whipped cream and pour into mould. Leave to set in refrigerator. Turn out on to serving dish and decorate with cherries and angelica. Serves four.

Blancmange or Cornflour Mould

Ingredients
1½ oz cornflour
1 pint liquid powdered non-fat milk
2 oz granulated sugar
1 teaspoon vanilla essence

Method
Blend the cornflour into a smooth paste with a little milk. Bring remaining milk to boil and pour on to the blended cornflour, stir well and pour back into the saucepan. Return to medium heat until mixture comes back to the boil, stirring all the time. Add sugar and essence and bring back to the boil again. Pour into a wetted mould and leave until set. Serves four.

Gooseberry Fool

Ingredients
1 lb green gooseberries
4 oz granulated sugar
¼ pint water
1 pint custard, made with custard powder and liquid powdered non-fat milk

c

Method
Top and tail gooseberries. Dissolve sugar in the water and put into the pan with the gooseberries. Stew until soft. Sieve and sweeten the pulp further if necessary. When cold mix with the custard and pour into individual glasses to set. Serves four.

Summer Pudding

Ingredients
4 slices bread
1 lb fruit (see note)
3 oz granulated sugar

Method
Stew the fruit with the sugar and let it cool. Trim the bread (the slices should be at least ½-inch thick). Line the bottom and sides of a 1-pint basin with bread, making sure the surface is completely covered. The fruit should not be too moist and should be pressed into the bread until the basin is full. Cover with a slice of bread and leave in refrigerator until quite cold and set. Turn out on to serving dish and serve with cold custard (made from powdered non-fat milk) or whipped cream (recipes pages 85–6). Serves four.

NOTE
The most usual fruits for this pudding are raspberries, red, black or white currants, blackberries and loganberries in various combinations.

Trifle

Ingredients
1 pint cold custard (made with custard powder and liquid
  powdered non-fat milk)
10 oz tin raspberries
½ sponge cake (recipe page 80)
2 to 3 tablespoons sherry
1 oz glacé cherries and angelica for decoration

Method
Cut sponge cake into slices and arrange in the bottom of a
glass dish. Add fruit, and sufficient juice to moisten sponge
cake, and spoon over the sherry. Lightly spread the custard
on to the trifle and decorate with cherries and angelica.
Serves four.

Rhubarb Crumble

Ingredients
1 large tin rhubarb
or
1 lb fresh rhubarb
3 oz granulated sugar
3 tablespoons water

CRUMBLE
3 oz crushed cornflakes
2½ oz caster sugar

2 rounded tablespoons powdered non-fat milk
2 oz self-raising flour
1 teaspoon brown sugar
3 tablespoons water

Method
If tinned rhubarb is used, drain off nearly all the juice before putting in a pie-dish. Fresh rhubarb should be washed, cut into 1-inch pieces and boiled with water and sugar. Allow to cool before adding the crumble, prepared as follows:

Crush cornflakes, add caster sugar, powdered milk and flour. Mix well with a fork. Gradually add the water, a tablespoon at a time, until the ingredients are damp. Spread on the rhubarb and sprinkle with brown sugar. Bake in a preheated oven (450 °F or Gas No. 8) for 25 minutes. Serves four.

Cherry Pie

Ingredients
15 oz tin cherry pie filling
4 rounded tablespoons plain flour
2 rounded tablespoons powdered non-fat milk
1½ level teaspoons baking powder
1 rounded tablespoon caster sugar
a pinch of salt
water to mix
(self-raising flour may be used instead of plain flour and
    baking powder)

Method
Sieve dry ingredients into a bowl and add a little water to

make a stiff dough. Line a floured pie plate with pastry and spoon on the filling and cover with another layer of pastry. Sprinkle with caster sugar and bake in a preheated oven (400 °F or Gas No. 6) for 20 to 25 minutes. Serves four.

Date and Apple Tart

Ingredients
2 large cooking apples
4 oz stoned cooking dates
2 rounded tablespoons granulated sugar
3 tablespoons water
4 oz icing sugar
2 teaspoons hot water
½ teaspoon lemon juice

PASTRY
4 rounded tablespoons plain flour
2 rounded tablespoons powdered non-fat milk
1½ level teaspoons baking powder
1 rounded tablespoon caster sugar
a pinch of salt
water to mix

Method
Peel, core and thinly slice apples. Place in a saucepan with the cold water, granulated sugar and chopped dates. Simmer until tender. Leave until almost cold, then sandwich date mixture between two layers of pastry, made as for Cherry Pie (page 68). Bake in a preheated oven (400 °F or Gas No. 6) for 20 to 25 minutes. When cold, cover with water icing made as follows:

Sieve the icing sugar into a bowl and gradually add the hot water and lemon juice until the mixture is of a spreadable consistency. Serves four.

Ground Rice and Blackcurrant Mould

Ingredients
1 pint liquid powdered non-fat milk
3 level tablespoons ground rice
2 rounded tablespoons granulated sugar
a pinch of salt
4 drops almond essence
3 tablespoons blackcurrant jam

Method
Pour ¾ pint milk into a saucepan, add salt and sugar and bring to the boil. Mix ground rice and essence into a smooth paste with the remaining cold milk. Pour boiling milk on to the ground rice, stirring well. Return to the saucepan over a low heat and boil, stirring continuously, for a few minutes until it thickens. Put the jam in the bottom of a wetted mould and carefully pour in mixture, allow to cool, and leave to set in a refrigerator. Turn out on to a dish. Serves four.

Blackcurrant Wheels

Ingredients
FILLING
6 tablespoons blackcurrant jam

PASTRY

4 rounded tablespoons plain flour

2 rounded tablespoons powdered non-fat milk

1½ level teaspoons baking powder

1 rounded tablespoon caster sugar

a pinch of salt

water to mix

(self-raising flour may be used instead of plain flour and
baking powder)

Method

Sieve the dry ingredients together and make into a soft dough
with a little water. Roll out into an oblong about ¼-inch thick.
Spread generously with jam and roll up as for Swiss roll. Cut
into six portions and lay in the bottom of an ovenproof dish,
and bake in a preheated oven (400 °F or Gas No. 6) for 20 to
25 minutes. Serve with custard (recipe page 86). Serves three.

Cakes

and sweet sauces

Angel Cake

Ingredients
2½ oz plain flour
6 oz caster sugar
a few drops vanilla or almond essence
5 large egg-whites
½ level teaspoon cream of tartar
a pinch of salt

Method
Sieve flour and 4 oz sugar together, three times, to aerate as much as possible. Place egg-whites, essence, cream of tartar and salt in a separate bowl and beat until a thick froth is formed. Gradually whisk in the remaining 2 oz sugar and continue to whisk until the mixture is very stiff and stands in peaks. Fold in the sieved flour and sugar as quickly as possible. Spoon mixture into an 8-inch non-stick cake tin and cut through several times with a knife to release any large air bubbles. Bake in the centre of a preheated oven (375 °F or Gas No. 5) for 35 to 40 minutes. Allow to remain in tin until cold. This cake can be eaten plain or sandwiched with jam.

Date and Cherry Squares

Ingredients
3 oz self-raising flour
1½ oz ground rice
2 oz powdered non-fat milk
3 oz stoned dates, finely chopped
3 oz Demerara sugar
1 dessertspoon golden syrup
1 egg-white
1 oz glacé cherries, finely chopped
a little liquid powdered non-fat milk

Method
Place dry ingredients in a bowl, add warmed syrup and lightly beaten egg-white with a little milk until the mixture is damp. Spread mixture on a non-stick baking tin or one lined with vegetable parchment, until it is about ½-inch thick. Bake in a preheated oven (375 °F or Gas No. 5) for 40 to 45 minutes until lightly brown and firm to touch. Cut into squares when cold. Makes 12 squares.

Quick Bread or Scones

Ingredients
1 lb plain flour
4 level teaspoons baking powder
3 rounded tablespoons powdered non-fat milk
1 level teaspoon salt
½ pint liquid powdered non-fat milk

Method

Mix dry ingredients together and add milk, forming mixture into a stiff dough. Knead lightly and quickly on a floured board. Cut and shape into 12 pieces and place on a floured baking sheet or leave in one piece and place in a 1-lb loaf tin. Bake in a preheated oven (425 °F or Gas No. 7) for about 20 to 25 minutes if in separate pieces or for 35 to 40 minutes as a single loaf.

Saffron Cake

Ingredients
6 oz saffron-flavoured flour
1 egg-white
2 oz caster sugar
1 oz dried currants
2 rounded tablespoons powdered non-fat milk
a pinch of salt
a little liquid powdered non-fat milk

Method

Sieve flour, sugar, powdered milk and salt together into a bowl, add currants and mix. Lightly beat the egg-white and stir in with a little liquid milk to make a soft consistency. Place in a small non-stick cake tin or one lined with vegetable parchment, and bake in a preheated oven (400 °F or Gas No. 6) for about 15 minutes. This cake will keep for three days.

Fruit Loaf

Ingredients
1 cup All-Bran cereal
1 cup caster sugar
1 cup mixed dried fruit
1 cup liquid powdered non-fat milk
1 heaped cup self-raising flour

Method
Put All-Bran, sugar and dried fruit in a mixing bowl and mix well together. Stir in milk and leave to stand for 1 hour. Sieve the flour and stir in thoroughly. Pour mixture into a non-stick loaf tin or one lined with vegetable parchment, and bake in a preheated oven (350 °F or Gas No. 4) for 1½ hours. This loaf will keep for up to four weeks.

Date Triangles

Ingredients
8 oz stoned cooking dates
4 oz plain flour
1½ level teaspoons baking powder
2 oz powdered non-fat milk
2 oz caster sugar
a pinch of salt
a little water
(self-raising flour may be used instead of plain flour and
    baking powder)

Method

Place the dates in a bowl and cover with boiling water. Allow to stand until cool and then beat with a fork. Flour an ovenproof pie plate. Sieve the dry ingredients into a bowl and add a little water to make a soft dough. Roll out half the pastry and place on the plate, spread the date mixture over and cover with the remaining pastry. Brush with liquid powdered non-fat milk and sprinkle with sugar. Place near the top of a preheated oven (425 °F or Gas No. 7) and cook for 20 minutes. When cool, cut into triangles. Makes about 12.

Jam Cake

Ingredients
4 rounded tablespoons plain flour
1½ level teaspoons Golden Raising Powder *or* baking powder
2 rounded tablespoons powdered non-fat milk
2 rounded tablespoons caster sugar
a little liquid powdered non-fat milk
jam for filling

Method

Mix all ingredients except jam together to form a soft dough. Then sprinkle an oblong baking tin with flour. Divide the dough mixture and roll out one half and spread on the baking tin, and cover with jam. Roll out remaining dough and place on top. Sprinkle with sugar and bake in a preheated oven (400 °F or Gas No. 6) for 20 minutes or until firm to touch. Eat the same day.

Macaroons

Ingredients
3 oz ground rice
3 oz caster sugar
1 egg-white
1 teaspoon almond essence
9 glacé cherries
about 1 teaspoon water

Method
Cover two baking sheets with rice paper. Mix ground rice and sugar. Beat the egg-white thoroughly and add to the dry ingredients with almond essence. Stir, adding the water until a stiff paste is formed. Spoon 9 equal amounts on to the baking sheets and press each into a flat shape, leaving room between to allow for spreading. Place a glacé cherry on each and bake in the centre of a preheated oven (350 °F or Gas No. 4) for 20 to 25 minutes. When cold trim off excess paper.

Rice Krispie Macaroons

Ingredients
2 egg-whites
1½ oz crushed Rice Krispies
1 teaspoon almond essence
2 oz caster sugar
glacé cherries
1 dessertspoon clear honey

Method
Prepare baking sheet with rice paper. Whisk egg-whites until very stiff. Add almond essence and honey and fold in sugar and Rice Krispies. Spoon on to rice paper and top each with a glacé cherry. Bake in a preheated oven (375° F or Gas No. 5) for 20 to 25 minutes. Makes 12 to 16 small macaroons.

Meringues

Ingredients
3 egg-whites
6 oz caster sugar

Method
Whisk egg-whites until very stiff. Add half the sugar gradually, whisking well after each addition. Fold in remaining sugar lightly. Cover an oblong baking sheet with rice paper and force meringue mixture into shapes with a forcing bag or two wet spoons. Dust with caster sugar and put into a cool oven for 2 to 4 hours (200 °F or Gas No. ½). Makes 10 to 12 meringues.

Nelson Squares

Ingredients
FILLING
4 thick slices bread, trimmed
3 rounded tablespoons dark brown sugar
1 level teaspoon mixed spice

3 drops vanilla essence
2 tablespoons dried mixed fruit
1 rounded tablespoon powdered non-fat milk
½ cup liquid powdered non-fat milk

PASTRY
6 rounded tablespoons plain flour
2 level teaspoons baking powder
2 rounded tablespoons powdered non-fat milk
2 level tablespoons caster sugar
a little water
(self-raising flour may be used instead of plain flour and
  baking powder)

Method
Soak the bread in the milk until it becomes soft and spongy.
Beat in the sugar, then add all other ingredients. Meanwhile
flour an oblong baking tin. Sieve the pastry ingredients
together and make into a soft dough with a little water.
Divide in half, roll out and cover tin. Spread over the filling
and cover with remaining pastry. Sprinkle with sugar and
bake on the middle shelf of a preheated oven (400 °F or Gas
No. 6) for 25 minutes. Cut into squares when cold. Will keep
for two days.

Potato Cake

Ingredients
½ packet dried potato (size to serve 3) made up with water *or*
3 rounded tablespoons cold mashed potato
2 oz caster sugar

2 rounded tablespoons plain flour
1 rounded tablespoon powdered non-fat milk
1 level teaspoon baking powder
½ cup dried mixed fruit

Method
Beat potato and sugar together until creamy. Sieve flour, powdered milk and baking powder together and add to the creamy mixture. Mix thoroughly and stir in the fruit. Turn into a floured 7-inch sandwich tin and level off. Bake near the top of a preheated oven (400 °F or Gas No. 6) for 30 minutes. Serve immediately.

Sponge Cake

Ingredients
4 oz plain flour
1 level dessertspoon custard powder
2 rounded tablespoons powdered non-fat milk
6 oz caster sugar
1 level teaspoon baking powder
3 egg-whites
jam for filling

Method
Beat egg-whites and sugar over a bowl of warm water until thick and creamy. Sieve flour, custard powder and powdered non-fat milk together and fold into mixture gently. Pour into two 8-inch non-stick sandwich tins and bake in the centre of a preheated oven (350 °F or Gas No. 4) for 20 to 25 minutes

or until firm. Leave for 5 minutes before turning out on to a cooling tray. Fill with jam.

Flapjack

Ingredients
4 oz rolled oats
2 oz Demerara sugar
2 oz self-raising flour
1 tablespoon clear honey
3 tablespoons water
2 rounded tablespoons powdered non-fat milk

Method
Mix all ingredients together. Spread mixture on a baking sheet lined with rice paper, to about ½-inch thick. Bake in a preheated oven (375 °F or Gas No. 5) for 25 to 30 minutes. Cut into squares when cool. Makes 12 squares.

Ginger Surprise

Ingredients
4 rounded tablespoons self-raising flour
½ level teaspoon ground ginger
1½ rounded tablespoons caster sugar
a pinch of bicarbonate of soda
1 egg-white
1 dessertspoon black treacle
1 tablespoon liquid powdered non-fat milk

FILLING AND TOPPING
7¾ oz tin fruit cocktail
2 tablespoons orange marmalade
whipped cream (recipes pages 85–6)

Method
Sieve dry ingredients together. Warm treacle and add with
whisked egg-white and milk. Mix thoroughly and bake in a
non-stick loaf tin in a preheated oven (375 °F or Gas No. 5)
for 20 to 25 minutes or until firm. Turn out on to a cooling
tray and allow to go cold. Drain fruit. Slice ginger cake
horizontally in half and spread with half the quantity of
whipped cream mixed with half the tin of fruit. Chop remaining fruit into small pieces and place in a saucepan with
marmalade and warm gently through. Pile mixture on top of
cake and decorate with remaining cream. Keeps for 3 days.

Marmalade Cake

Ingredients
6 oz self-raising flour
3 oz Demerara sugar
2 oz powdered non-fat milk
1 tablespoon orange marmalade
1 oz chopped candied lemon peel
3 tablespoons liquid powdered non-fat milk
1 egg-white
a pinch of salt

Method
Sieve flour, powdered milk and salt together. Add 2½ oz sugar

and lemon peel. Whisk egg-white until frothy, and add to mixture with the marmalade. Stir in liquid milk and mix well. Place mixture in a small non-stick loaf tin and sprinkle with remaining sugar. Bake in a preheated oven (375 °F or Gas No. 5) for 30 minutes.

Christmas Cake

Ingredients

5 oz self-raising flour
3 oz Demerara sugar
½ teaspoon mixed spice
4 drops rum essence
1 dessertspoon black treacle
a pinch of salt
½ lb mixed currants and sultanas
1 oz chopped candied peel
1 oz glacé cherries, halved
2 egg-whites
2 tablespoons powdered non-fat milk
1 dessertspoon marmalade
3 tablespoons liquid powdered non-fat milk

MOCK ALMOND PASTE

4 oz semolina
4 oz icing sugar
1 egg-white
2 teaspoons almond essence

Method

Sieve flour, powdered milk, spice and salt, add sugar, fruit, peel and cherries. Whisk egg-whites until frothy and add to the mixture. Spoon in the treacle, marmalade and essence and stir well. Lastly, add the liquid milk. Line a 6-inch cake tin with vegetable parchment and spoon in the mixture. Bake in a preheated oven (375 °F or Gas No. 5), reducing heat to 350 °F or Gas No. 4 when cake is placed in oven. Bake for 45 minutes. When cold, cover with mock almond paste, made as follows:

Mix dry ingredients together and stir in the whisked egg-white and almond essence. Cover with icing as desired.

Crushed Pineapple and Cherry Cake

Ingredients
8 oz self-raising flour *or*
8 oz plain flour and 3 level teaspoons baking powder
2 level teaspoons ground ginger
4 oz caster sugar
3 oz powdered non-fat milk
2 egg-whites
16 glacé cherries
4 tablespoons liquid powdered non-fat milk
13¼ oz tin crushed pineapple
a pinch of salt
angelica (optional)

Method
Sieve the dry ingredients together. Stir in 2 tablespoons strained crushed pineapple and 8 quartered cherries. Fold stiffly beaten egg-whites into the mixture with the liquid milk. Place mixture in a non-stick 7-inch cake tin and bake in a

preheated oven (350 °F or Gas No. 4) for 1 hour. Allow to cool and pile remaining crushed pineapple on top. Decorate with cherries and angelica.

Substitute Whipped Cream (1)

Ingredients
1 rounded tablespoon powdered non-fat milk
1 average-size banana
1 egg-white
4 drops vanilla essence

Method
Slice banana into small thin pieces and then add the powdered milk, essence and egg-white. Beat thoroughly until stiff.

Substitute Whipped Cream (2)

Ingredients
1 pint liquid powdered non-fat milk
a pinch of salt
½ oz gelatine
2 rounded tablespoons powdered non-fat milk
1 rounded tablespoon custard powder
2 to 3 oz caster sugar (according to taste)
3 drops vanilla essence

Method
Dissolve the gelatine in a little water in a bowl standing in a

pan of warm water over moderate heat. Then add the powdered milk and the custard powder blended with 4 tablespoons of liquid milk. Heat the remaining milk, adding a pinch of salt, until it is boiling, and stir into mixture in basin. Return to pan and boil for 1 to 2 minutes. Add the sugar and essence. When mixture is cold but not set, whisk thoroughly until the cream has risen considerably and is light. Chill before using.

Substitute Whipped Cream (3)

Ingredients
2 rounded teaspoons cornflour
½ pint liquid powdered non-fat milk
1 oz caster sugar
flavouring (if desired)
2 rounded tablespoons powdered non-fat milk

Method
Blend the cornflour with a little cold milk. Heat the remaining milk in a saucepan. Add to the cornflour and return it to the pan and boil for a few minutes. Set aside to cool. Cream the powdered milk, sugar and flavouring together with a little liquid milk. Gradually beat in the thick cornflour mixture and continue to beat until creamy.

Custard

Ingredients
2 rounded tablespoons custard powder

2 oz caster sugar
1 pint liquid powdered non-fat milk

Method
Blend the custard powder and sugar together with a little milk. Bring the remaining milk to the boil and pour on to the blended custard powder and sugar. Stir well and pour back into the saucepan. Return to medium heat until mixture thickens and comes back to the boil, stirring all the time.

Brandy Sauce

Ingredients
1 small wineglass (or up to 4 tablespoons) brandy
½ pint liquid powdered non-fat milk
½ oz cornflour
1 oz sugar

Method
Blend the cornflour and sugar with a little milk to form a paste. Heat remaining milk and pour on to mixture, stir thoroughly and return to heat. Simmer gently until sauce thickens, add brandy, stir and serve.

Glossary of English Terms with some American Equivalents

The following equivalents and explanations may be useful to anyone not familiar with English usage.

Angelica	The candied stem and root of an aromatic plant used for decorating cakes, puddings, etc.
Baking powder	American baking powder may be stronger than the British variety and less will be needed—possibly only half the amount specified
Basin	In these recipes, a pudding bowl in which the pudding can be boiled or steamed
Beef	'Skirt' or 'Chuck' of beef signifies stewing steak; 'topside' is akin to rump roast
Bicarbonate of soda	Baking soda
Black treacle	Molasses may be substituted
Butter beans	Large, dried white-seeded beans similar to Lima beans
Caster sugar	Fine granular, white sugar suitable for use in a sugar caster or sifter—used because it blends and dissolves more readily than coarser sugars

Channel Island milk	Milk from the Jersey and Guernsey breeds of cattle which is especially rich in milk fat
Chicken joint	A complete limb of a chicken—a chicken piece
Cornflour	Cornstarch
Custard powder	Proprietary item based on cornstarch and containing no eggs or milk fat
Demerara sugar	A golden-coloured crystalline form of sugar
Dried herbs	A mixture of dried, savoury herbs—a typical example might contain sage, thyme, marjoram and pennyroyal
Flour	Where plain flour is specified all purpose flour should be used. In Britain, self-raising flour contains added baking powder. 'Saffron flour' is a proprietary item coloured and flavoured with saffron. 'Seasoned flour' in these recipes means flour to which salt and pepper have been added before using it
Frying pan	Skillet
Glacé cherries	Candied, whole, stoned cherries
Golden Raising Powder	A proprietary brand of coloured baking powder
Golden syrup	A sugar syrup more highly refined than black treacle, *q.v.*
Gravy browning/ powder	A proprietary item for thickening and colouring gravy
Ground rice	A granular form of rice flour
Icing sugar	Confectioners' sugar
Loaf tin	Bread baking tin

Minced meat	Ground meat (not to be confused, of course, with mincemeat described on p. 59)
Mixed fruit	Dried raisins, currants and sultanas, *q.v.*, bought ready mixed
Mixed peel	Candied orange and lemon peel bought mixed and chopped ready for use
Mixed spice	The common spices bought ready ground and mixed. A typical example might contain cinnamon, coriander, dill, fennel, nutmeg, ginger, clove, turmeric
Packet of jelly	Fruit-flavoured gelatine in crystalline or cake form which only needs to be dissolved in boiling water
Patty tin	A tin for baking a batch of small pies or cakes each in its own mould—a cupcake tin
Plaice	A small, white-fleshed, flat fish found in coastal waters
Sandwich tin	A 'layer cake pan' either round or oblong
Spring onions	Very young, seedling onions eaten raw in salads
Sultana	A dried, seedless raisin, originally from Smyrna, usually lighter in colour than ordinary dried raisins
Tart	Usually, an open fruit pie
Worcester sauce	A proprietary bottled sauce used for flavouring stews, etc.—Worcestershire sauce
Whiting	A small, white-fleshed sea fish

Weights and Measures

The American, and also the metric, equivalents of the British weights and measures used in these recipes are given below.

Liquid Measures

The fluid ounce (fl oz) is the same in both Britain and America
  The British (or Imperial) pint = 20 fl oz
  The American pint   = 16 fl oz

Measuring cups (liquid measure)
  British breakfast cup   = 10 fl oz ($\frac{1}{2}$ Imperial pint)
  British teacup   = $6\frac{2}{3}$ fl oz ($\frac{1}{3}$ Imperial pint)
  American standard cup   = 8 fl oz ($\frac{1}{2}$ American pint)

Standard measuring spoons (liquid measure)
The American standard tablespoon and standard teaspoon are slightly smaller than their British equivalents.
  8 British standard tablespoons = 5 fl oz
  10 American standard table-
    spoons   = 5 fl oz
  In each country, 3 teaspoons   = 1 tablespoon
  1 British dessertspoon is approximately $\frac{1}{2}$ to $\frac{2}{3}$ of a tablespoon

Approximate Metric Equivalents

Liquid measures

1 fl oz	= 28 millilitres (ml)
1 British (Imperial) pint	= 570 ml
1 American pint	= 450 ml
1 litre	= 1¾ Imperial pints
	= 2⅕ American pints

Weights

1 ounce (oz)	= 28 grams (g)
1 pound (lb) (16 oz)	= 454 g
1 kilogram (kg) (1000g)	= 2 lb 3 oz

Table of measurements for certain dry ingredients using American standard cup and tablespoon.

	Weight in ounces contained in:	
Ingredient	*1 cup*	*1 level tablespoon*
Sifted flour	4	¼
Caster sugar	7	½
Confectioners' or icing sugar	4½	¼
Syrup, Treacle, Molasses	12	¾
Rice (whole grain)	7½	½
Currants	5½	–
Fresh breadcrumbs	2½	–
Cornstarch or cornflour	–	⅓

Index